To Ted and Ernie,
Turn the page and take a look,
A story's like a dream in books!
Love
Aimée x
CW00868278

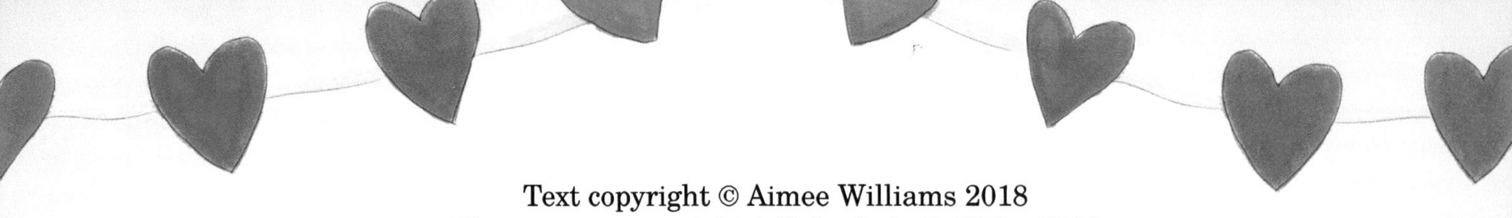

ISBN: 978-1-911569-66-4

First published 2018
by Rowanvale Books Ltd
The Gate
Keppoch Street
Roath
Cardiff
CF24 3JW
www.rowanvalebooks.com
Library Cataloguing in Publication Data.
A catalogue record for this book is available from the British Library.

To my Princess, my Angel and my Little Star. This one is for you.
Thank you for being my inspiration, my joy, and my world.
xxx

To my husband, my parents, my family and friends - thank you for your unconditional support and encouragement. And to my husband and 'Big Sis' for always being my 'on-call' proof readers!
xxx

Faith and the Tooth Fairy

Faith had lost another tooth,
This wasn't the first time,
In fact, she'd lost a lot of teeth,
And this was number nine!

When Faith went up to bed that night,
She had a job to do,
Tonight she'd have a visitor,
Who'd come and take her tooth.

So she lifted up her pillow,
And she placed her tooth beneath,
Knowing that the Tooth Fairy
Would come when she's asleep.

She'd never met the Fairy,
But she always dreamed she would,
She thought, *Maybe if I stay awake,*
Tonight, I really could!

Then suddenly, to her surprise,
A very quiet sound...
So she slowly pulled the covers back
To take a look around.

And then upon her pillow
Was a sprinkling of dust,
And above it was the fairy,
Who was smiling as she blushed.

"I've never stirred a child before,
I'm sorry, Faith," she said.
"You know my name?" Faith asked, surprised,
Then sat upright in bed.

"Of course I do! Each child I see,
I know them all by name.
Each one of you is special,
And not one of you the same."

"I have a question," Faith replied,
"Where do the teeth all go?
I wondered what you do with them—
I'd really like to know."

"Sometimes," said the Tooth Fairy,
"Parents write to me,
And they ask if I can leave a coin,
But also leave the teeth.

"I suppose they like to have them,
As a keepsake for their child,
So I write it in their journal.
Every child has a file!

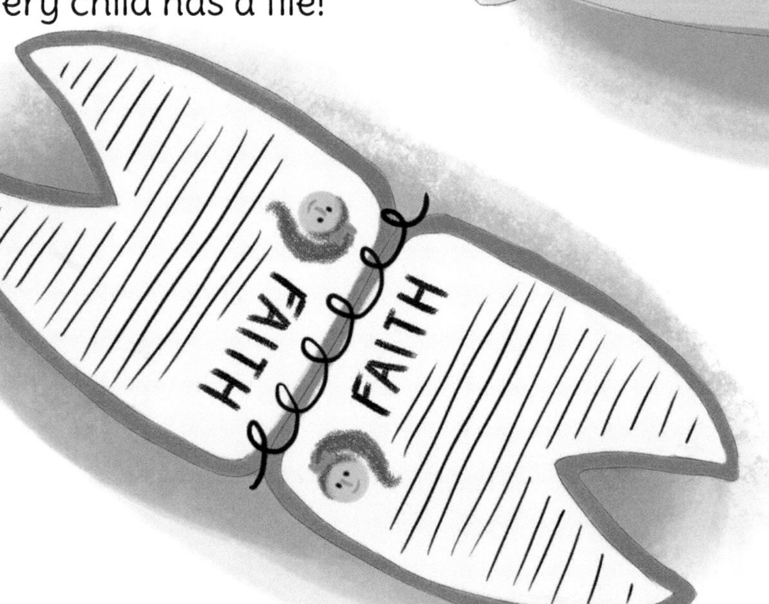

"But all the other teeth I take
To Tooth Town in the sky.
Would you like to come and see
it now?"
But Faith said, "I can't fly!"

"With just a little fairy dust
And happy thoughts, you can!"
Then out the window, off they flew,
Together, hand in hand.

They flew so high above the clouds,
Faith could see the moon.
"It's not far now," the Fairy said,
"We'll be there very soon!"

And sure enough, beyond the clouds
(It hadn't seemed that far),
Was a little place called Tooth Town,
Hidden in amongst the stars.

It was beautiful and colourful,
A rainbow way up high.
Faith said, "I've never seen so many
Stars up in the sky!"

The Fairy said, "They're special stars;
Look closely and you'll see,
Every single one of them
Is made from little teeth.

"I bring the teeth to Tooth Town,
As I know how great they are,
Then a little bit of magic,
And I turn them into stars!

"There's my house," the Fairy said,
"The bricks are all so white."
"I bet it's made from teeth," Faith said.
"Of course it is—you're right!"

"But come with me, there's more to see,
I've saved the best for last;
We cross the stream, go through the trees,
Then straight along this path."

"And here it is, the place I work,
It's where I get my power.
It's oh so white, and big and bright,
The magic Toothy Tower!"

The sun was setting in the sky,
And morning soon would come.
It was time for Faith to get back home;
She'd had a lot of fun.

They flew back down together,
And Faith went back to bed.
"Thanks for my adventure,
It was wonderful," she said.

Soon it was the morning.
Faith woke and wasn't sure
If she'd really met the Fairy,
Or just dreamt the night before.

She lifted up her pillow,
And she found a coin so fine,
And a note left by the fairy,
Saying: *Faith, until next time...*

When Elijah went to bed at night,
He'd always have a dream.
His mind would take him places
That you never would believe.

On Sunday he was up in space,
He took off from his room,
He met some friendly aliens,
Had tea up on the moon!

He flew around the planets
And played leapfrog over stars,
His rocket went to Venus,
Then to Saturn, then to Mars!

On Monday he went sailing
Right across the seven seas,
He found some hidden treasure
That belonged to Pirate Pete!

Had a parrot on his shoulder,
And a little wooden leg,
A red and silver eyepatch,
And a hat upon his head!

On Tuesday he was climbing
Up a mountaintop so high,
He passed the clouds until he reached
A rainbow in the sky,

He climbed upon the rainbow,
Then he took a look around.
He closed his eyes then slid back down,
Until he hit the ground!

On Wednesday he went on the train,
To London, all alone,
He met the Queen, had jam and tea,
She showed him round her home!

He went to the museum,
And he stood beneath Big Ben.
He went up on the London Eye,
Then went on it again!

Thursday was exciting,
As he found himself in Spain—
He learned he was a pilot,
It was he who flew the plane!

He learned to dance flamenco,
Ate paella by the sea,
He learnt to count in Spanish
(Well, he got to number three!).

Come Friday, he was riding
On a ladybird, so small,
He had shrunk and lived with fairies,
He was less than one inch tall!

He could talk to creepy-crawlies,
The spiders and the ants,
He went and had a boogie
At the annual insect dance!

On Saturday he went to France,
A beret on his head,
But he wasn't speaking English,
He was speaking French instead!

Bonjour, comment allez-vous?
(Hello, and how are you?),
Comment t'appelles-tu?
À bientôt (See you soon)!

It's safe to say Elijah
Had adventures every night;
He travelled all around the world,
And saw so many sights!

So now it's time for you to sleep,
I bet you're keen to see
Where your mind decides to take you,
As you close your eyes and dream!

A Little Old Rabbit Named Woof

Kailah had a rabbit, and she named her rabbit Woof.
She was a baby when she got him, so found speaking rather tough—

But woof was a word she'd mastered, so it soon became his name,
She knew no rabbit in the world could ever be the same.

Woof would go where Kailah went; she rarely left him home,
She knew with Woof she had a friend, she'd never be alone.

He always went to school with her; he hid
inside her bag.
Kailah said her bunny was the best friend
that she had.

He sat with her at breakfast and
beside her in the car,
She cuddled him at bedtime; he
was never very far.

When she had her bedtime stories and
her goodnight lullabies,
Woof would sit there listening, a twinkle
in his eyes.

She would kiss him as she lay in bed,
and cuddle him in near,
But Woof was so well loved, he grew a
hole beneath each ear!

Kailah felt so sad that Woof had poorly, broken ears;
She asked her mummy kindly, as her eyes welled up with tears,

"Can you sew him back together, please? Make him good as new?"
Her mummy said, "Of course I will. I know just what to do!"

When Kailah went to bed that night, her rabbit wasn't there,
He wasn't on her pillow and he wasn't in the chair.

"Where are you, Woof?" poor Kailah cried. "I need you here," she said,
"It's getting late, the stars are out—it's time to go to bed!"

But Woof was nowhere to be seen; she thought that he was lost,
She looked all round the house for him, she even searched the loft!

Then thought that maybe Mummy had been tidying her room—
Perhaps she'd cleaned the floor and he'd got swept up by the broom.

"He might be in the dustbin getting grubby, oh, the stink!
I'd have to wash and clean him lots, with bubbles in the sink!

"Or maybe he has come to life and gone out for a walk,
But lost his way and couldn't say... if only Woof could talk!

"Or perhaps he's on a journey, and he'll be back very soon,
He may be on an aeroplane, or even on the moon!

"Maybe he got hungry and he went to get some food,
But he never goes; he always knows to stay here in my room!

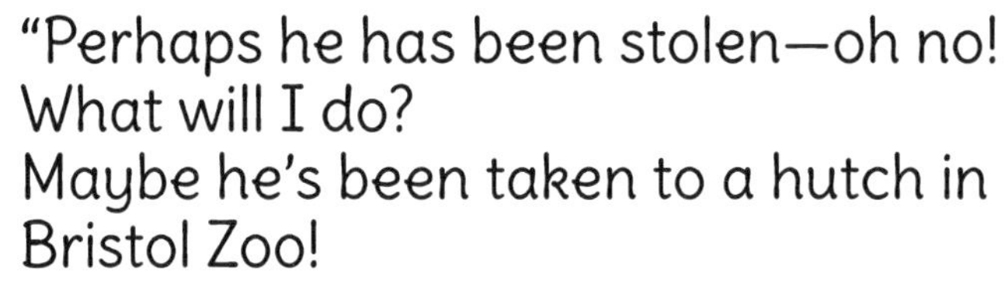

"Perhaps he has been stolen—oh no! What will I do?
Maybe he's been taken to a hutch in Bristol Zoo!

"Perhaps my Woof is magic and he's
playing tricks on me,
He's made himself invisible; he's here,
but I can't see?!

"Maybe he got frightened while I left him on his own.
But I only went to Grandma's, so he knew I'd soon be home!

"What if he tried to follow me, I didn't even know,
He couldn't go as fast as me; his feet were far too slow?

"He really could be anywhere," Kailah said, and sighed,
"I'll never get to sleep if Woof's not here
with me tonight."

And then a noise outside her room;
she shouted out, "Who's there?"
It was just her mummy's footsteps;
she was coming up the stairs.

“Oh, Mummy, help me!” Kailah said, “I think Woof’s disappeared.”
“Now look, come see, he’s here with me; I’ve fixed his broken ears!”

Kailah was so happy, and she found it rather funny,
Her rabbit hadn’t vanished; he was simply with her mummy!

Woof was good as new again; all the holes were sewn.
Kailah now could go to sleep, no longer on her own.

“Goodnight, my darling,” Mummy said. “I’ll now turn out the light—
Goodnight, Woof, now have sweet dreams; close your eyes, sleep tight.”

Author Profile

Aimee Williams is 35 years old and lives with her husband and three children in Bristol. She has been writing poetry from a very young age and has always dreamed of having her work published for others to read and enjoy. These three stories were written for and inspired by her children.

For more information about Aimee and the bespoke poetry business she runs, please visit www.aimeewilliams.co.uk.

Publisher Information

Rowanvale Books provides publishing services to independent authors, writers and poets all over the globe. We deliver a personal, honest and efficient service that allows authors to see their work published, while remaining in control of the process and retaining their creativity. By making publishing services available to authors in a cost-effective and ethical way, we at Rowanvale Books hope to ensure that the local, national and international community benefits from a steady stream of good quality literature.

For more information about us, our authors or our publications, please get in touch.
www.rowanvalebooks.com
info@rowanvalebooks.com

Lightning Source UK Ltd.
Milton Keynes UK
UKIC03n2306270418
321792UK00003B/17
* 9 7 8 1 9 1 1 5 6 9 6 6 4 *